*For Tade, who makes me merry*
*all year long —A.W.P.*

*Especially for Grayson and Ella.*
*Merry Christmas! —D.W.*

Farrar Straus Giroux Books for Young Readers
An imprint of Macmillan Publishing Group, LLC
175 Fifth Avenue, New York, NY 10010

Text copyright © 2018 by Ann Whitford Paul
Pictures copyright © 2018 by David Walker
Color separations by Bright Arts (H.K.) Ltd.
Printed in China by Toppan Leefung Printing Ltd.,
Dongguan City, Guangdong Province
Designed by Roberta Pressel
First edition, 2018
1  3  5  7  9  10  8  6  4  2

mackids.com

Library of Congress Cataloging-in-Publication Data

Names: Paul, Ann Whitford, author. | Walker, David, 1965- ill.
Title: If animals celebrated Christmas / Ann Whitford Paul ; pictures by
David Walker.
Description: First edition. | New York : Farrar Straus Giroux, 2018. |
Summary: Rhyming text explores what would happen if animals celebrated
Christmas like humans do, from a penguin and chick writing letters to
Santa to a koala and her parents sharing a holiday cuddle.
Identifiers: LCCN 2017036965 | ISBN 9780374309015 (hardcover)
Subjects: | CYAC: Stories in rhyme. | Christmas—Fiction. | Animals—Habits
and behavior—Fiction. | Parent and child—Fiction.
Classification: LCC PZ8.3.P273645 Ifm 2018 | DDC [E]—dc23
LC record available at https://lccn.loc.gov/2017036965

Our books may be purchased in bulk for promotional, educational, or business use.
Please contact your local bookseller or the Macmillan Corporate and Premium Sales Department
at (800) 221-7945 ext. 5442 or by e-mail at MacmillanSpecialMarkets@macmillan.com.

# If Animals Celebrated Christmas

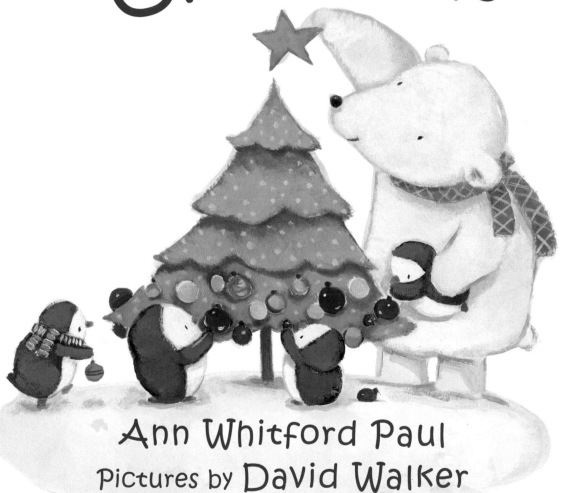

Ann Whitford Paul

Pictures by David Walker

Farrar Straus Giroux

New York

If animals celebrated **Christmas**,
Koala, high in a tree, would cheer,

"**Christmas is coming!
It's almost here!**"

Tortoise would tuck in his head and **hissssssssssssssss**, making a secret holiday wish.

Penguin and Chick would slowly float,
writing letters to Santa on their icy floe boat.

The bells on Oryx's horns would ring,
*Ting, ting-a-ling! Ting-a-ling-ling!*

If animals celebrated **Christmas**,
Koala and Mama would lazily drape
their tree with long strands of berries and grapes.
Then they'd ask Owl, "Can you fly up high?
Our top needs a star plucked from the sky."

Beaver would gnaw,
**gnaw-gnaw**,
trees with his teeth,
breaking off branches for a holiday wreath.

Hedgehog would purr and knit-knit with her quills

a sweater for Hoglet with fancy frills.

If animals celebrated **Christmas**,
Koala would stir, helping Papa make
a yum-yum leafy, Santa-shaped cake.

Crabs would scamper from the deep, dark sea,

and build a seashell Christmas tree.

Papa and Mama Buffalo

would grunt greetings and kiss beneath mistletoe.

Crane carolers would flap-flap their wings.

"Hark, we blessed birds all sing!"

If animals celebrated **Christmas**,

Koala would hang up her stocking

and cuddle
with Mama and Papa—
**a holiday huddle**.

Then she'd fall asleep in her high-branch bed
with visions of reindeer flying through her head—
a team of them!—fast on their way,

pulling Polar Bear Santa in his gift-heavy sleigh.

"Ho! Ho! Ho! Merry Christmas!"

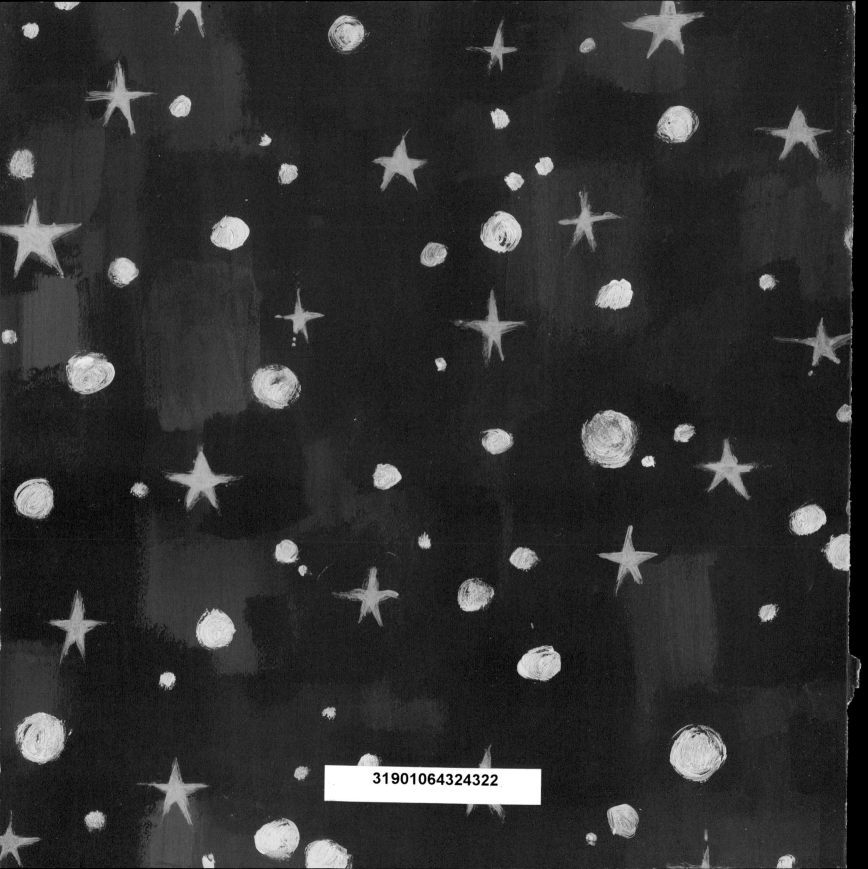